KT-404-831

A catalogue record for this book is available from the British Library.

First edition

Published by Ladybird Books Ltd Loughborough Leicestershire UK

© 1993 The Walt Disney Company
All rights reserved. No part of this publication may be reproduced, stored in a retrieval system, or transmitted in any form or by any means, electronic, mechanical, photocopying, recording or otherwise, without the prior consent of the copyright owner.

Printed in EC

Disney

Peter Pan

Ladybird Books

Deep in the heart of London there was a house where the Darling family lived.

Wendy Darling shared a big nursery with John and Michael, her two young brothers. At bedtime, she would tell them stories about a faraway place called Never Land, where a boy named Peter Pan lived.

The boys believed that Peter Pan was real, and they made him the hero of all their nursery games.

One night, while their parents were getting ready to go out for the evening, John and Michael were playing together as usual.

"Take that, Peter Pan!" cried John, lunging at his brother with a toy sword. Michael fought back and they leapt from bed to bed as they continued their fierce duel.

The boys were making so much noise that their father, who was struggling to knot his tie, went storming into the room to quieten them. Mr Darling was in such a bad temper that he blamed Wendy for all the commotion. "You shouldn't stuff their heads with this silly nonsense about Peter Pan!" he thundered. "It's about time you grew up, young lady. From now on you will have your own room. This is your last night in the nursery. Do you understand?" And with that, he stomped out of the room, slamming the door shut behind him.

Later that night, Peter Pan and his fairy companion Tinker Bell flew in through the nursery window. Peter had come to recapture his shadow, which had escaped one night while he had been listening at the window to one of Wendy's stories.

But the shadow was feeling mischievous and didn't want to be caught. It skipped across the wall just out of Peter's grasp. Wendy tried to help, but Tinker Bell, who was in a spiteful mood, tugged at Wendy's hair to keep her back.

Peter finally caught up with his naughty shadow. Wendy, who was delighted to meet her hero at last, offered to sew it back in place.

"I'm so glad you came tonight, or I might have missed you," said Wendy. "This is my last night in the nursery. Father says it's time for me to grow up."

Peter was horrified. "Come with me to Never Land," he urged. "You'll never have to grow up there."

"How will we get there?" asked Wendy.

"We'll fly, of course!" said Peter. He sprinkled the children with golden pixie dust and told them to think happy thoughts.

The children did as they were asked and soon, much to their surprise, they were soaring high above the rooftops of London.

14

They flew all night. At last
they saw the enchanted world
of Never Land far below.

"Look!" cried Michael.
"A pirate ship!"

On board the ship was Captain Hook, Peter Pan's greatest enemy. Once, in a fair fight, Peter had cut off the pirate's left hand and fed it to a hungry crocodile. The crocodile had liked the taste of it so much that he had followed Captain Hook ever since, hoping for a chance to finish off the snack.

Captain Hook couldn't believe his luck when he saw Peter and the children in the sky above. He barked an order at one of the pirates. "Load the cannon, Mr Smee. We'll pot them like sitting ducks!"

The cannonball went whistling through the air, missing the children by inches.

"Quick, Tinker Bell," said Peter. "Take Wendy and the others to the island while I draw Hook's fire!"

Now Tinker Bell was growing more and more jealous of Wendy. Peter Pan seemed to like this girl far too much.

Without waiting for the others, Tinker Bell flew straight to Peter's hideout beneath Hangman's Tree to rouse the Lost Boys.

The spiteful fairy let the
Lost Boys know that a
terrible Wendy Bird was
heading their way, and that
Peter had ordered them to
shoot it down.

Grabbing their clubs and
catapults, the Lost Boys
raced outside to ambush
the dreadful beast.

As the children were flying overhead, the Lost Boys shot poor Wendy out of the sky with stones from their catapults. Luckily, Peter came swooping down just in time to save Wendy from crashing.

Peter Pan was furious with the Lost Boys. "But Tinker Bell said your orders were to shoot her down," they protested.

To punish Tinker Bell, Peter banished her for a week. She crept off into the forest feeling very sorry for herself.

Peter was eager to show Wendy the island, but Michael, John and the Lost Boys wanted to do something far more adventurous. Peter decided to leave John in charge. "Go and capture some Indians," he ordered.

John bravely led his men across the island in search of their prey.

At last the boys came to a small clearing in the middle of a wood, and John explained his plan. "We simply surround the enemy and take them by surprise."

Unfortunately, John didn't get the chance to put his plan into action. The Indians, who had disguised themselves as trees, crept up on the boys and seized them before they knew what was happening.

The Indian braves took the boys back to their village and tied them to a big totem pole.

John and Michael were beginning to get worried.

"It's all right," said the Lost Boys reassuringly. "The Chief will let us go."

But they were wrong. The Chief's daughter had disappeared and the Chief was convinced that the Lost Boys knew where she was. "Unless Princess Tiger Lily is returned by sunset, you will be burnt at the stake," he threatened.

Meanwhile, Peter and Wendy were exploring Mermaid Lagoon.

A little rowing boat appeared in the distance. As it drew closer Peter could see the occupants.

"It's Hook!" he cried. "He's captured Princess Tiger Lily and is heading towards Skull Rock. Let's see what he's up to."

Peter and Wendy climbed onto a high ledge. They saw
Captain Hook tie Tiger Lily to a rock near the shore.

"If you don't tell me where Peter Pan's hideout is," they heard him snarl, "I'll leave you here to drown when the tide comes in!"

Poor Tiger Lily was very frightened, but she bravely refused to talk. Peter Pan was her friend. She would never betray him.

Peter didn't wait to hear any more. He flew straight down to save Tiger Lily.

"Peter Pan!" howled Captain Hook, drawing his sword. Peter landed on the blade and bounced up and down on it as if it were a spring. The vibrations shook Captain Hook right through to his bones.

Up and down the rocky cliffs they fought until Captain Hook lost his footing and almost fell into the sea. He just managed to hook onto a rock to save himself. Down below he could see the crocodile, his jaws open wide.

The crocodile was determined that Captain Hook should not escape him. He leapt from the water and clamped his sharp teeth into the Captain's jacket, pulling him down into the water.

"Hang on, Captain. I'm coming!" shouted Mr Smee, rowing as hard as he could.

Peter was so busy laughing at the crocodile's antics that he completely forgot about Tiger Lily. It wasn't until Wendy reminded him of the danger the Princess was in that he dived into the sea to save her.

Rising out of the water with Tiger Lily in his arms, Peter watched as Mr Smee and Captain Hook headed back to their ship, with the crocodile following a short distance behind.

The Chief was so relieved
to see his daughter safe and
well that he made Peter an
honorary chief.

The boys were set free and soon joined in a huge celebration. Whooping with delight, they danced round the totem pole to the beat of tom-tom drums.

At last, exhausted by all their adventures, Peter and the children returned to their secret hideout.

Word had reached Captain
Hook that Peter had banished
Tinker Bell. He sent Mr Smee
to fetch the fairy to his pirate
ship.

Tinker Bell was deep in
thought and didn't notice Mr
Smee creeping up behind her.
She was still brooding over
Wendy and blamed Peter for
bringing her to Never Land.

"Pardon me, Miss Bell," said
Mr Smee, popping his cap over
Tinker Bell. "Captain Hook
would like a word with you."

Captain Hook welcomed
Tinker Bell aboard his ship and
explained that he wanted to
capture Wendy and make her
into a servant to scrub and cook
for the pirates. All Tinker Bell
had to do was to show him
where Peter's hideout was so he
could find Wendy.

Tinker Bell was only too
pleased to help. She dipped her
toes in ink and danced across a
map of Never Land. Her
footprints led straight to
Hangman's Tree.

"Thank you so much, my
dear," said Captain Hook.
Then he grabbed Tinker Bell
and locked her in a lantern.

Back at Peter's headquarters, John, Michael and Wendy were beginning to get homesick.

"I want my mother," sobbed little Michael.

The Lost Boys joined in. But they soon brightened up when Wendy said they could *all* return home with her.

Peter was upset when he heard that his friends wanted to leave, but he didn't try to stop them. "Just remember," he warned, "once you leave Never Land, you can *never* come back."

Wendy was the last to leave. "Goodbye, Peter," she said. "I'll never forget you."

But the pirates were lying in wait and captured the children as they emerged from the hideout. Wendy, her brothers and the Lost Boys were tied up with ropes and carried off into the dark forest.

Before returning to the ship, Captain Hook placed a parcel on Peter's doorstep. It had a label on it that read, *To Peter with love from Wendy*.

The children were tied to the main mast of the ship. The crew danced round them. "Come and join us," they urged. "You'll love the life of a pirate!"

At the far end of the deck sat Captain Hook. "Either join my pirate band, or walk the plank," he snapped. "The choice is up to you."

The boys quite liked the idea of being pirates and rushed to sign up. But Wendy refused. "Peter Pan will save us," she said.

Mr Smee and Captain Hook began to chuckle. "I'm afraid Peter Pan won't save you this time," sneered the Captain. "We left him a surprise package. It contains a bomb. Very soon, Peter Pan will be blasted out of Never Land for ever."

On hearing these words,
Tinker Bell began to struggle
and kick inside the lantern.
Suddenly there was a *crack!*
and the glass broke. Tinker Bell
was free! Forgetting all about
her jealousy she flew off to
warn Peter Pan.

Peter was examining the parcel with interest when Tinker Bell arrived. He gasped with astonishment as Tinker Bell wrenched the package from his grasp. Seconds later a huge explosion shook the ground and Peter's hideout was reduced to rubble.

Peter searched frantically through the wreckage. "Where are you, Tinker Bell?" he called.

Luckily, Tinker Bell was dazed but unharmed. She quickly warned Peter that Wendy and the others were in great danger.

Meanwhile, back on the pirate ship, Captain Hook had lost patience and had ordered Wendy to walk the plank. Her head held high, she bravely stepped off the end.

Everyone held their breath
and waited for the *splash!* as
she hit the water. But the
splash never came. Peter Pan
arrived just in time to scoop
Wendy to safety.

"Oh, Peter! I was sure you
would come," Wendy told him.

Peter set Wendy down on the deck and turned to face his enemy. "Say your prayers, Hook!" he cried, drawing his dagger.

There was a loud clash of steel as Peter and Captain Hook locked weapons. Back and forth they fought, to the sound of cheering from the children.

Breaking free, Peter flew to the very top of the pirate ship. Captain Hook climbed up after him and they continued their duel on the rigging.

Hook lunged at Peter, missing him by inches. Peter regained his footing, but the Captain lost his balance and toppled backwards.

The crocodile, who was waiting below, licked his lips.

This time, there was a loud *splash!* as Captain Hook hit the water. Desperately, he began swimming towards Mr Smee's little rowing boat.

The children cheered and cheered. Then Peter gave the order to raise the anchor and Tinker Bell scattered the pirate ship with her golden pixie dust.

The ship soared high in the air over Never Land and floated on towards London.

In next to no time the children were back home.

When Mr and Mrs Darling returned home after their evening out they found the children gazing out of the nursery window.

"Oh, Mother!" cried Wendy. "We had such wonderful adventures in Never Land."

"Now Wendy," said her father, "you know there's no such place…"

"Look!" cried Wendy, pointing to the sky. "There's Peter Pan's ship!"

Her parents could scarcely believe their eyes, for above them they saw the ghostly outline of a pirate ship silhouetted against a full moon.

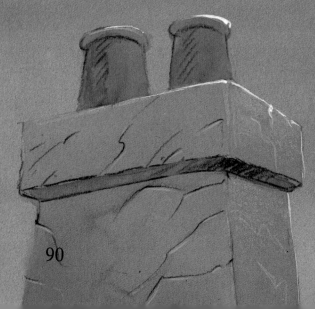

And even Mr Darling –
who was a practical man –
had to admit that Peter Pan
really *did* exist – but only if
you believed in him.

ABCDEF